JR: to Corinna
LS: to Gwenda

GABBA GABBA WE ACCEPT YOU

THE WONDROUS TALE OF JOEY RAMONE

by JAY RUTTENBERG
illustrated by LUCINDA SCHREIBER

DRAG CITY
CHICAGO

In New York City, many moons ago, a baby greeted the world.
It was spring, when the air itself feels like magic: the season of hope.
The baby's parents, filled with the bountiful love that all parents
feel for their children the second they meet them,
named their son Jeffrey.

JEFFREY ROSS
HYMAN.

The world is packed with
such delights as SPAGHETTI...
and French POODLES...

and those WONDROUS moments when all the people in your family start laughing at the same time.

But life can also be challenging. And for Jeff, challenges came early.
For he was born sick.

When other new babies are cuddling with their mothers and fathers,
Jeff was with doctors, who labored to make him feel better.

It is a great pleasure to inform you that the doctors succeeded. Soon enough, the baby was back where all babies belong, cuddling with his parents.

The family moved to Forest Hills, Queens, where the hectic city meets the leafy suburbs.

Yankees

Now, here's ANOTHER *MIRACULOUS* THING:

Every person on earth is a little bit different from every other person on earth. Weird, right? Sometimes a person's uniqueness is obvious; sometimes it stays hidden.

Jeff's differences were the obvious kind. In a country where most people are Christian, his family was Jewish. At a time when most kids didn't wear glasses, he was prescribed thick frames.

He was thin and ungainly, and even ran in a manner that other children found funny. Gym class was never his friend.

Everybody feels too *something*. And mostly, Jeff felt too tall. When you feel too tall, there's no hiding.

Soon enough, bullies—UGH! ICK! YUCK! ACHHH!—spotted this thin, clumsy, incredibly tall kid and, with devil's instinct, smelled difference.

Difference: the pathetic lifeblood of all bullies. Did they tease Jeff because of his height? Yes, they most certainly did. It was the lowliest, most vicious form of bullying—picking on a gentle person not for what they do, nor for what they say, but for what they are. The bullies were mocking Jeff for existing.

"Whoa whoa whoa whoa!"
you must be thinking.
"This is a

But remember all that stuff about
the world being packed with
INCREDIBLE
THINGS?

Well, here's one more
mind-blowing creation:

MUSIC.

One opportune day when Jeff was young, he happened upon a wild noise that would forever alter his life. It was the kind of sound that makes those who hear it want to simultaneously sing and laugh and cry and shout and jump around like they are...

...TOTALLY, ABSOLUTELY, POSITIVELY BONKERS.

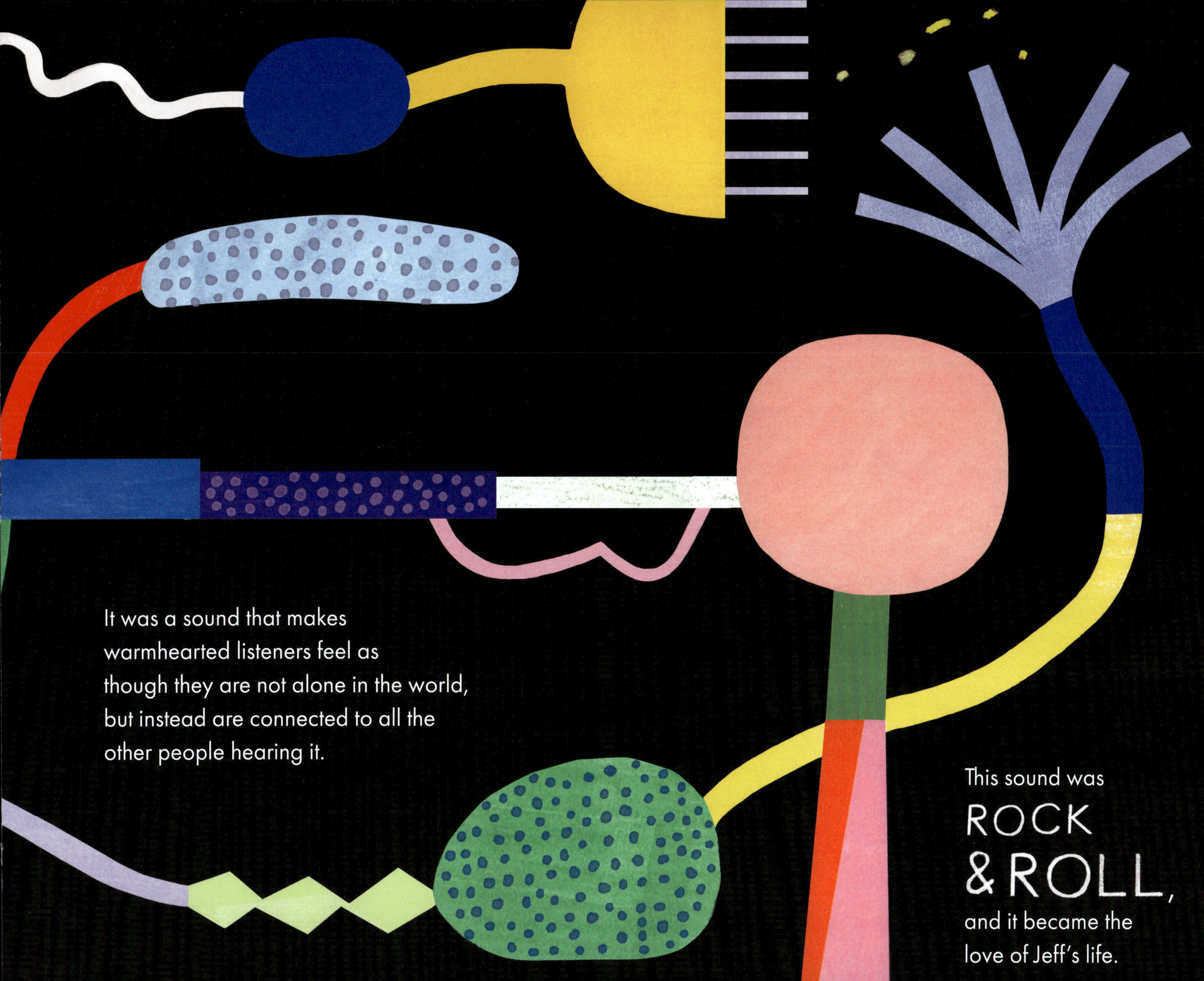

It was a sound that makes warmhearted listeners feel as though they are not alone in the world, but instead are connected to all the other people hearing it.

This sound was

ROCK

& ROLL,

and it became the love of Jeff's life.

In time, this tall, frail, quirky child became a tall, frail, quirky young man. Although he was a grown-up, Jeff still felt like a kid. He had yet to find his

SUPER POWER

—the little bit of MAGIC buried deep inside each person that lets the world catch a glimpse of the greatness lurking within us all.

Jeff's heart still beat to the frenzied pulse of rock & roll. But the music had changed. The rock songs that Jeff had first fallen in love with sounded like they were created by kids after they had eaten way too much birthday cake and were running around like maniacs while their parents yelled,

"STOP ACTING SO CRAZY YOU CRAZY KIDS!

THE PARTY'S OVER AND IT'S ***TIME TO GO HOME*** AND TAKE A BATH WHILE I LECTURE YOU ABOUT ***TOOTHBRUSHING!***"

By the time Jeff became a grown-up, rock music sounded like it was being made by the parents. This was a problem. And while he didn't know it yet, Jeff was destined to solve it.

Jeff started playing in a band with some friends from the neighborhood. At first, he played drums. Then one day it was decided, without much fanfare, that Jeff should try singing.

The year was 1974. Rock & roll had already been around for about twenty years. Nearly a century had passed since Thomas Edison had invented the phonograph, capturing the sound of the human voice.

And when did people start singing? More than 500,000 years prior. That's an awfully long time—even before your grandparents were born.

But in all of those years—and through all those millions of singers—nobody had *ever* sounded like Jeff.

RAMONES

His singing was at once heartbreaking and funny, friendly but also a little tough—because New York back then could be a pretty tough place.

His bandmates' instruments complemented his voice perfectly. A great band deserves a great name, and they gave themselves one:

THE RAMONES

The four musicians all assumed new names for the band. John Cummings, the guitarist, became Johnny Ramone. Bassist Douglas Colvin was now Dee Dee Ramone. Thomas Erdelyi, who took over playing drums from Jeff, was christened Tommy Ramone.

And what of Jeffrey Hyman? He was now the mighty lead singer of the Ramones, celebrated the world over as Joey Ramone.

C.B.G.B.
RAMONES
TALKING HEADS
BLONDIE
AT CBGB'S June 17,18,19
CBGB
315
OMFUG
315
Rob
wuz
Here

TAKE IT DEE DEE

At Ramones concerts, Joey would take the stage with his bandmates.

All the musicians were dressed in the same uniform—blue jeans, leather jacket, T-shirt, sneakers—but each was a fierce individual, distinct from his fellow Ramones.

Joey would peek through his ridiculous mass of hair and spy a happy audience cheering him on.

In the crowd, some people felt too tall and some too small, some too timid, some too restless, and some simply too kooky.

"Take it, Dee Dee!" Joey would say to his bassist. "1, 2, 3, 4!" Dee Dee would yell.

GABBA
GABBA
WE ACCEPT
YOU

Then the music would begin. It was a racket; to hear it was to dance to it. "Gabba gabba we accept you!" Joey would chant in "Pinhead," one of the band's most beloved songs. "We accept you one of us!"

And as the Ramones performed, all the differences in the room would melt away. All were united—all were Ramones.

The music the band played resembled the rock & roll they had grown up with, but it was presented with a weird and energetic new twist. Soon, listeners gave a funny name to the Ramones' music:

PUNK

A lot of people think that being a punk means acting crude or looking goofy or being just like the Ramones. They are wrong. It actually means something much simpler: Being your own person. Doing what *you* want to do, instead of doing what you think other people want you to do.

27

This was the splendor of Joey Ramone.
He was always Jeffrey Hyman—awkward, tall, shy Jeffrey Hyman, who was born sick, who spent years being taunted by bullies, who so often felt out of place and uncomfortable. But Jeff never curved to the world.

Jeff *CURVED* the world to him.

If you are ever in New York City, head to East 2nd Street and the Bowery, a cozy corner at peace with the madness around it.

It's right by what was once CBGB, the club where the Ramones often performed, and also close to where Jeff lived when he was a grown-up. Now look up and marvel at what the street sign reads: "Joey Ramone Place." Because while the Ramones no longer walk the earth, the earth still bears their footprints.

PLEASE

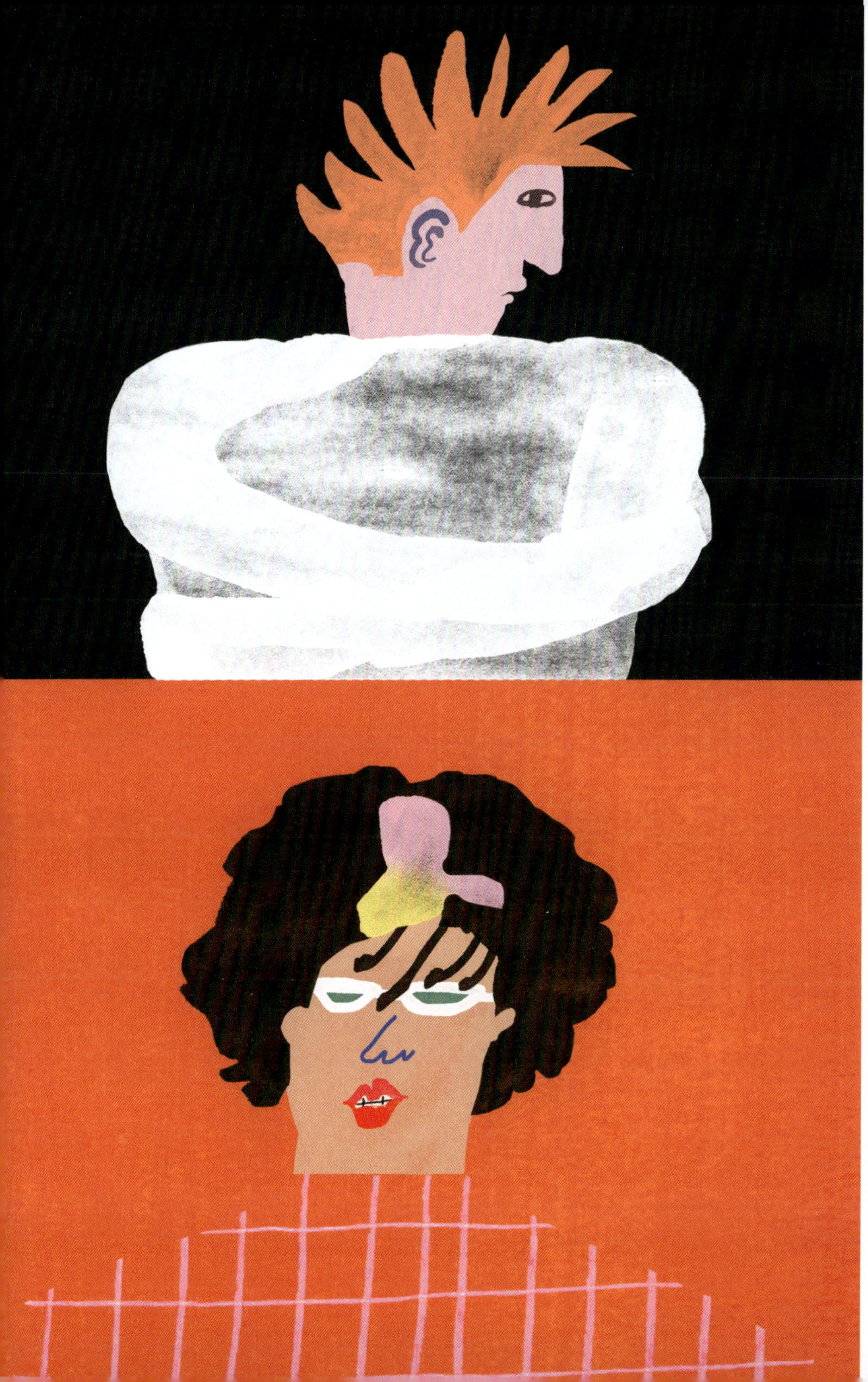

The punk rock that they birthed kept going—year after year, decade after decade—each new act a unique entity within the Ramones' cosmos.

In New York, punk included the wild-eyed poetics of Patti Smith and Richard Hell, the ornate guitars of Television, the dance songs of Blondie. Punk quickly migrated across the Atlantic Ocean to London, lighting the spark of a gazillion British bands including the Clash, Buzzcocks, X-Ray Spex, and, most famously, the Sex Pistols.

Punk headed west to Los Angeles... and to South America...and to Australia...and beyond.

Punk kept growing and twisting, always inspiring creative young people to express themselves. And then, one very special day, it reached you. Yes, you, silly! Go grab a pen or a marker or something. It's time to make up a song! If you are too little to write, just ask a grown-up to jot down whatever you say.

Writing a song is not complicated—it can be about *anything*. In fact, many of the greatest Ramones lyrics revolve around words you probably say every day:

"I WANNA!"

OK, are you ready?
Take it, Dee Dee!

1,2,3,4!

Acknowledgments:

JR: Thank you to Corinna, Francesca, my parents, and all the lovely people at P.S. 11, Children's Garden, and, of course, the inimitable Drag City. Also, thank you to the Ramones. Grown-ups can read more about the band in *I Slept with Joey Ramone*—the terrific memoir by Joey's brother, Mickey Leigh, written with Legs McNeil—and in *Please Kill Me*, the fascinating oral history of punk written by McNeil and Gillian McCain.

I got to see the Ramones perform only once, just before closing time (Brixton Academy, London, 1996). But of course, their music permeates all that follows it, and lives on eternally in the present. The Ramones serve as the glorious exclamation point at the end of rock & roll's arc—but they are also the point of entry to the music's charmed second act. Joey Ramone, forever.

LS: Many thanks to Jason and Anna for being my collective sounding board, to my mother for her unwavering support, and to my father and brother for their infectious love of music. But most of all, thank you to Jay and Drag City for entrusting me with this, and to the beacon that was and is Joey Ramone; his unparalleled spirit shines on through the music of so many who came after him, and hopefully through the pages of this book.

Jay Ruttenberg is the editor of the comedy journal the *Lowbrow Reader* and of the book *The Lowbrow Reader Reader*. He has written for the *New Yorker*, the *New York Times*, and other publications. He grew up in suburban Chicago and lives with his family in New York City.

Lucinda Schreiber is an award-winning illustrator and animator. She has collaborated with a long list of clients, including MoMA, Saks Fifth Avenue, the BBC, NPR, and Vox. Born in South Africa and raised mostly in Australia, she currently resides in Brooklyn.

Request to make copies of any part of this work should be mailed to:
Drag City Incorporated
Attn: Permissions Department
P. O. Box 476867
Chicago, Illinois 60647-6867
or e-mail to:
info@dragcity.com

Words by Jay Ruttenberg
Illustrations by Lucinda Schreiber

Copyediting and proofreading by Allison Dubinsky

DC936

www.dragcity.com

ISBN: 978-1-937112-42-4